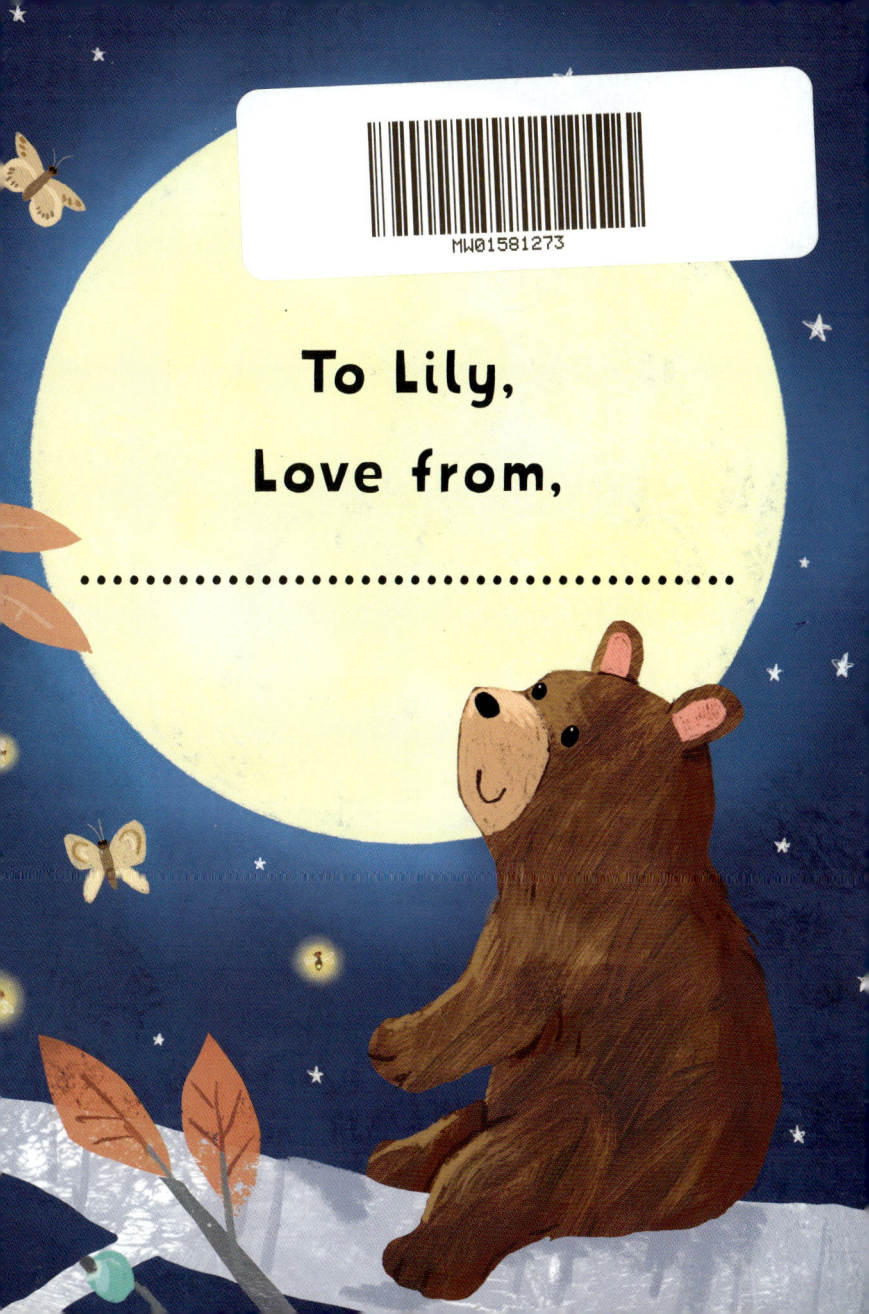

"Sweet little Lily,
time to shut your eyes.
The moon has come out,
there are stars in the skies."

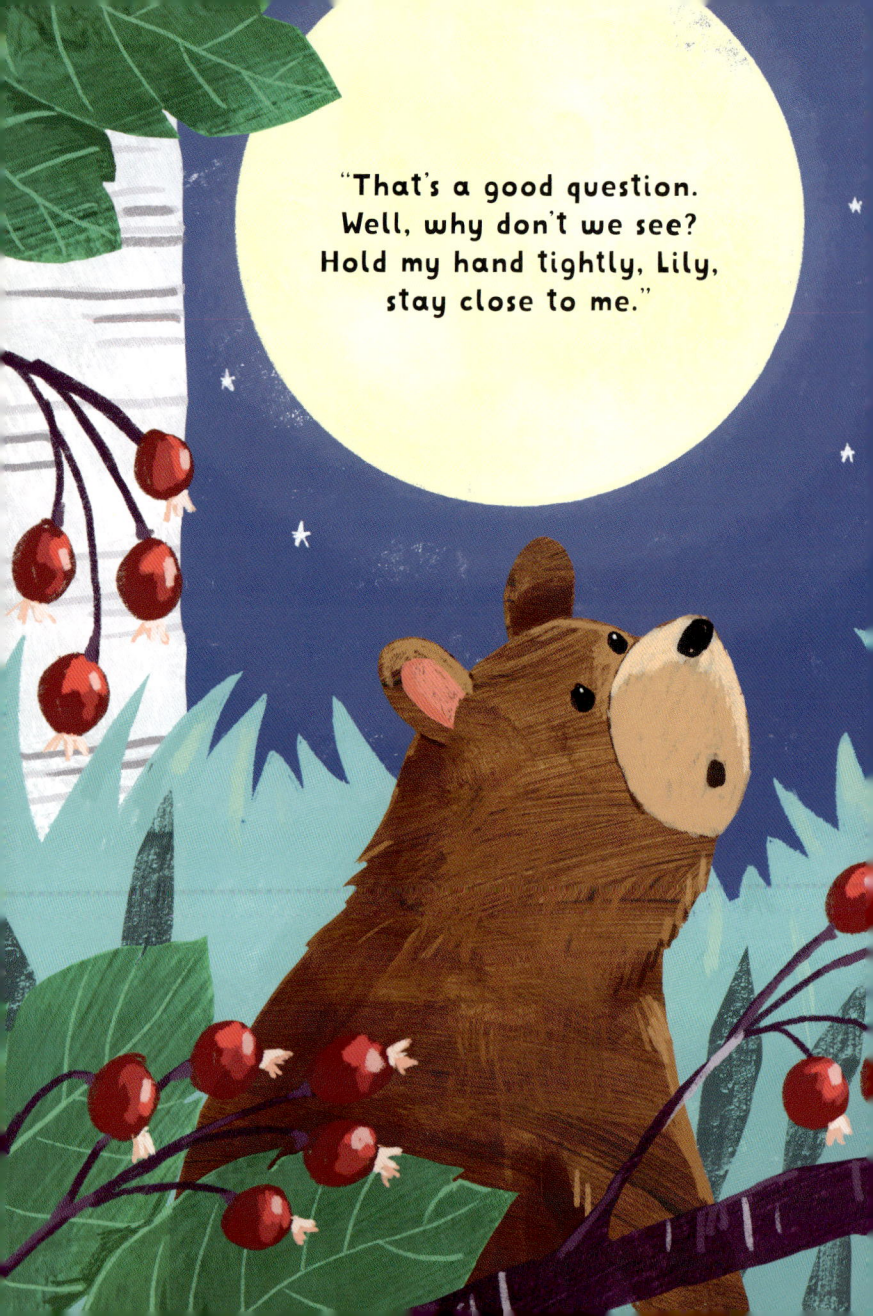

"Deer share happy thoughts.
It makes them all smile.
They'll settle down
then be asleep
in a while."

"These hedgehogs are S-T-R-E-T-C-H-I-N-G
It's the start of their day.
At bedtime they'll end it
the very same way!"

Lily's Countdown to Bedtime

10 Put away your toys

9 Take a bath

8 Brush your teeth

7 Use the bathroom

6 Wash your hands

Written by J.D. Green
Illustrated by Joanne Partis
Designed by Ryan Dunn

Copyright © Bidu Bidu Books Ltd. 2024

Put Me In The Story is a
registered trademark of Sourcebooks.
All rights reserved.

Published by Put Me In The Story,
a publication of Sourcebooks.
P.O. Box 4410, Naperville, Illinois 60567-4410
(630) 536-1104
putmeinthestory.com

Date of Production: July 2023
Run Number: 5032755
Printed and bound in China (GD)
10 9 8 7 6 5 4 3 2 1